THE MIGHTY MAGICAL

MOON
PALS

S0-CTA-790

Illustrations were done by Zachary Gladwin
The storyboard was created by Avery Ota
The story was written by John Fiorentino

Copyright © 2020 by John Fiorentino and Fio Companies.
All rights reserved. No part of this book may be reproduced or
used in any manner without the written permission of the copyright
owner except for the use of quotations in a book review.
For more information, address: info@moonpals.com.

Identifiers: ISBN 978-1-7355075-1-4
www.MoonPals.com

THE MIGHTY MAGICAL

MOON
PALS

AND THE HUGS THAT SAVED THE WORLD

Created by John Fiorentino

Illustrated by Zachary Gladwin

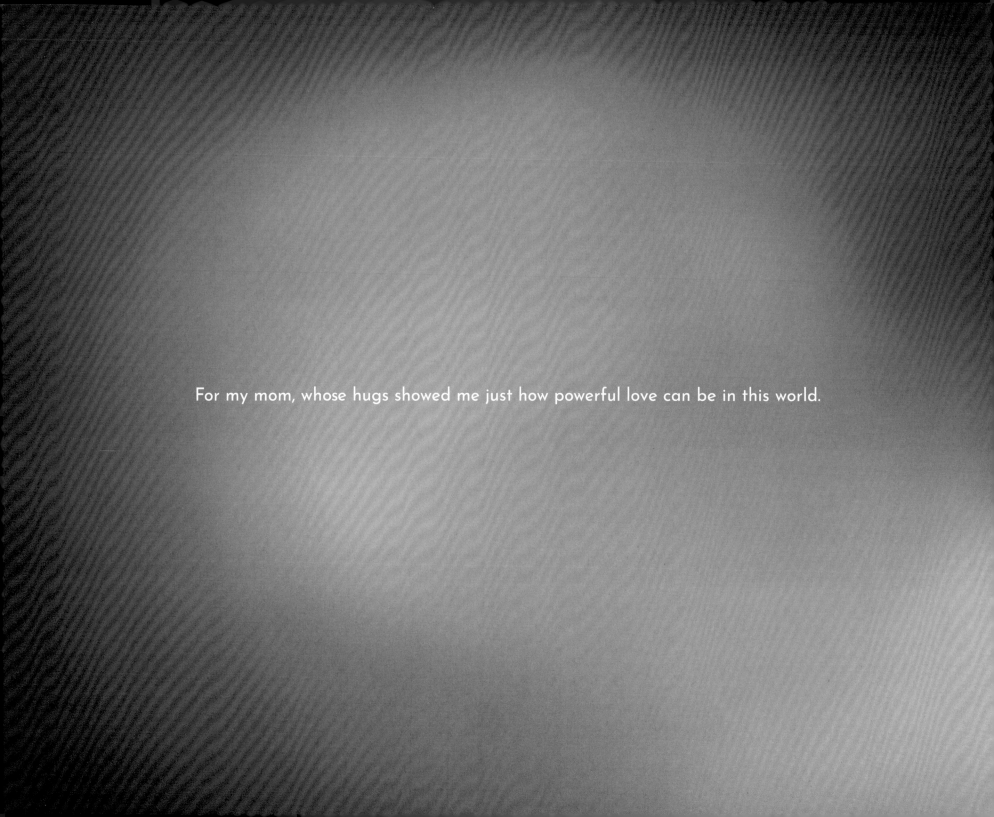

For my mom, whose hugs showed me just how powerful love can be in this world.

Look up at the Moon!
See how brightly she shines in the night?
Legend says that her light is not just any light.
It holds magical, mystical powers...

For she is Mother Moon,
Her warm glow is the key to all life.

And if you gaze at her just long enough,
You might feel a small fizzle or a tiny spark.
Her energy lives in your heart, keeping you, and
every being, calm and safe.

One night, a long time ago,
Mother Moon was watching over Earth,
shining her Magical Moon Energy down below.

Her bright light glowed with peace and quiet,
comforting Earth's creatures, as they ended the day.

Suddenly, a strange shadow crept in.
It silently spread across the night sky,
blocking each star, one by one.

It was the powerful Shadow King!
He was jealous of Mother Moon's mystical glow
and the happiness she created below.

"How dare Earth be so peaceful—
I must put an end to this!" he exclaimed.

The Shadow King had one simple plan:
to rule the world with his evil forces
and fill the night with loneliness and despair.

He swept his shadow across Mother Moon,
blocking her Magical Moon Energy, until Earth lost its light.

With the Moon Energy now gone,
Earth's creatures became sad and hopeless.

Mother Moon couldn't bear to watch,
she had to defeat the Shadow King before it was too late!

"I must do something to stop this!" she exclaimed. "I need to find a way to sneak past the Shadow King and bring my Magical Moon Energy back to Earth!"

Suddenly, she had an idea!

She mixed a pinch of moondust with a splash of starlight, stirring in as much Magical Moon Energy as she could.

And with a thundering boom...

The Mighty Magical Moon Pals were born!

Brave Mylo came first,
bursting with honesty and courage.

Gentle Echo was next,
filled with patience and compassion.

Clever Nova came third,
gifted with curiosity and intelligence.

Creative Opal followed,
granted with hope and imagination.

Kind Bo was last,
flowing with peace and understanding.

The Moon Pals were mighty, but were they mighty enough to
stop the Shadow King and save Earth's creatures?
To be sure, Mother Moon reached deep into her heart and gave each
Moon Pal a drop of her strongest Magical Moon Energy yet...

...love.

With a simple, loving hug, they could now turn any darkness into light.

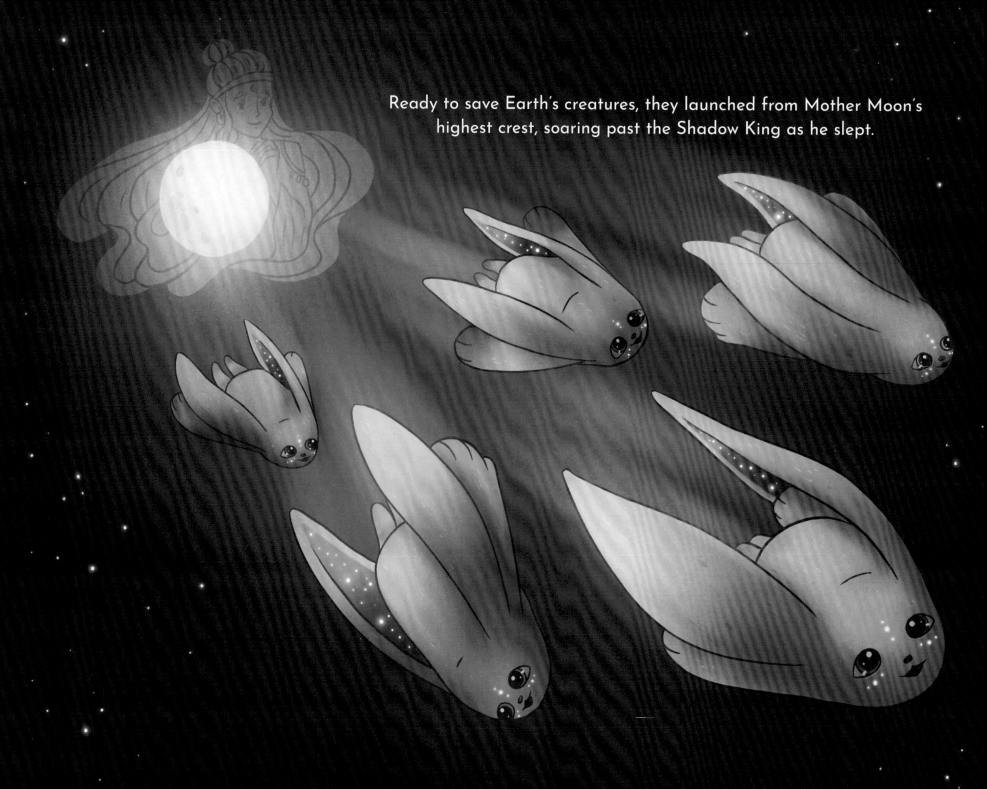

Ready to save Earth's creatures, they launched from Mother Moon's highest crest, soaring past the Shadow King as he slept.

With love in their hearts, the Moon Pals landed on Earth, ready to heal with their hugs.

They hugged and hugged,
spreading Magical Moon Energy near and far.

They warmed the sad, lost, and lonely hearts,
filling each one with love.

And just like that, Earth's creatures were calm and smiling once again.
They slept soundly in their beds as peace returned to Earth.

"It looks like all the creatures are happy again!" said Mylo. "It's time to make our way back to Mother Moon!"

"But wait!" Nova exclaimed.
"These hugs won't last. To keep Earth peaceful, we
need to stop the Shadow King for good!"

The Shadow King suddenly appeared and
laughed at the Moon Pals—
"Your powers are no match for me!
I will block the Magical Moon Energy forever!"

"Remember the most important power Mother Moon gave us," whispered Opal, "Love!"

"There IS still one creature we haven't hugged..." said Mylo, taking the lead.

"Echo agreed, "That's right! One who needs it more than anyone!

"To hug the Shadow King we goooo!" shouted Bo.

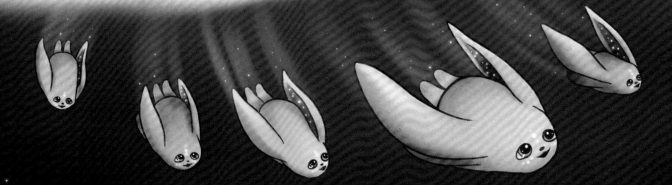

The Moon Pals mustered the rest of their strength to give the Shadow King their mightiest and most magical hug of all!

Together, they wrapped their arms around him, squeezing so tight that he couldn't resist.

As love entered his cold heart, it started to glow,
radiating with peace and kindness.

Full of light, he swept up his shadow and returned to his galaxy, promising to never again disrupt Earth and its creatures.

Mother Moon could once again
shine down on Earth,
all thanks to the Moon Pals
and their mighty magical hugs.

She couldn't have been more proud of her Moon Pals!

And anointed them as special guardians of her energy
and Earth's magical protectors forevermore.

Ever since that night, The Mighty Magical Moon Pals fly forth together, spreading love near and far with their magical hugs.

Now, when you gaze up at the night sky and see a soft glow,

you can be sure Mother Moon and her
Moon Pals are working hard to keep you safe.

And remember, if you ever feel sad or scared, there's no need to worry.

Your Moon Pal is always here to give you your very own Mighty Magical Moon Pal Hug!

Sara Marshall, Avery Ota, Zachary Gladwin, Jarrett Lerner, Denise and Joe Fiorentino, David Walker, James Levy, Hannah Zisman, Sara Baldoni, Alex Adelman, Ajay Mehta, Ashwin, Matt Cauble, Laurel Lee Derby, and everyone else who I texted nonstop for three years bouncing ideas off them.

Authors Note:

I've always tried to create things that make people happy. After creating the Gravity weighted blanket and Moon Pod, it became clear how powerful and helpful the right product could be in someone's life. I wanted to take the weighted therapy I had discovered to be so powerful and create something to help, in my opinion, the most important people on the planet: children. I wanted to wrap this powerful product in a magical world where kids could let their imaginations run wild, help them understand how to conquer their own fears, and show them how powerful love can be in this World. Hugs were such an essential part of my life growing up, and I can't imagine a better story to tell children than one about the power of a loving hug. The Mighty Magical Moon Pals are the superheroes I wish I had growing up, and I hope everyone enjoys them as much as I have had the pleasure of creating this fun, magical, loving World over the past few years. Thank you for joining us on this journey, and we are thrilled to welcome you to the Mighty Magical World of Moon Pals.